Capri

A One Act Play

Roger Bonner

Tortive Lit

First published in 2024 by Tortive Lit.

Tortive Lit is a part of Tortive Theatre Ltd.

The Straw Yard, Parade, Berwick-upon-Tweed, TD15 1PB

hello@tortivelit.com

www.tortivelit.com

ISBN: 978-1-7396920-6-3

Contents

1

Introduction

The inspiration to write *Capri* came from a trip to Italy many years ago. At the time, I was staying on Ischia and went on a day trip by boat to Capri along with swarms of tourists. Besides the spectacular beauty of the island, I was struck by the song "Isle of Capri" which was played constantly in all the souvenir shops. I escaped the throng of other tourists by going to the very northeast part of the island. As I wandered alone among the ruins of the Emperor Tiberius' *Villa Jovis*, I envisioned Capri as the ideal setting for a short play about a crime writer plagued by writer's block, and a young woman visiting him to avenge the murder of her sister. The play finally came to fruition when **The Semi-Circle Theatre** in Basel, Switzerland, called for submission of short plays, and accepted *Capri* for performance in 2021.

Roger Bonner

2024

2

First Performance & Production

Capri was first presented at the Festival of European Anglophone Theatrical Societies in 2023 in Bad Homburg, Germany and was directed by Samantha Levitt.

Adrian Fuller

Rik Deurloo

Marissa Portland

Alannah Burns

It was nominated for **Best Original Script** and Alannah Burns was nominated for **Best Actress**. The production won the Discretionary Award for its Ending Visuals.

* * *

CHARACTERS

Female Identifying Characters

Marissa

Male Identifying Characters

Adrian

3

Production Notes

From her entrance until the point where she plays with her hair (Medusa scene), Marissa Portland should gradually transition from being awe-struck and seductive to menacing. Especially in the Medusa scene, it is important that she slowly lifts strands of her hair to simulate writhing snakes.

The end of the play with its twist must come as a complete surprise. There should be a long pause with the light slowly fading while the song *'Twas on the Isle of Capri* is played once more, but this time mournfully. Ideally a recording by Marissa or another singer can be played without an orchestral accompaniment. Then the lights suddenly go on and Adrian wakes from his dream to find the perfect end for his novel.

4

Capri

A One Act Play

ADRIAN is sat at his desk in the middle of typing. He finishes, sits back and then reads what he has written.

ADRIAN: She walked about the room, stopped, and stared at him sitting there... (*pause*) and...and...AND?!

He sighs deeply in frustration looks at the bottle of wine and pours more into the glass, then takes a deep gulp. He puts the glass down and goes to type. His fingers hover over the keyboard. He can think of nothing. He takes another large gulp of wine. He picks up the phone and dials.

Hi, Nigel? It's Adrian. Look, I'm going to need another couple of days. Yes...yes...I know we said that today was the last deadline...but...I'm...well...stuck. Yes...stuck...for Christ's sake Nigel, you're a literary agent, you should know what 'stuck' means!

Louder strains of the song "'Twas on the Isle of Capri", sung by Frank Sinatra, are now coming through the window.

'Twas on the Isle of Capri that I found her

Beneath the shade of an old walnut tree

Oh, I can still see the flowers blooming round her

Where we met on the Isle of Capri...

ADRIAN: *(Annoyed and struggling to concentrate on what Nigel is saying)* Yes…yes…I know the publisher has set a deadline for the book! Yes, I am listening to you…it's just that they're playing that blasted song again. *(He moves towards the audience and shouts.)* Will you turn that bloody thing off! *(Returning his attention to Nigel.)* How many versions are out there? Dean Martin, Fats Domino, Bing Crosby, Frankie Lane, Frank Sinatra…on and on. I hate this version the most! *(Pause)* Calm down, Nigel! I know the publisher is after you too. *(Pause; pacing in circles)* I am working on it now and I'll try and get it to you a week from today.

The song stops playing and ADRIAN notices something through the window.

Another bloody boat from Naples has just arrived…disgorging its cargo of mindless day-trippers. Look at them swarming about the Piazzetta, all eager to buy their kitschy souvenirs and silly T-shirts. *(Pause)* No, I'm not being a *prima donna*. *(Gets up and starts pacing nervously about the room)* I've had a bit of writer's block, that's all. Look I promise you that I'll get it to you on Monday. When have I ever let you down before? *(Pause)* Same to you, Nigel, ciao.

He goes back to the desk, sits down, and concentrates again on his writing. He continues typing. The doorbell rings. ADRIAN ignores it. It rings again. (Shouts.) Just a moment. (He gets up and puts the bottle and glass on top of the sideboard; stares at the glass.)

Gulps the rest of the wine and places the empty glass next to the bottle, then goes stage right and opens the door. MARISSA wearing Capri pants, blouse, and as mid-size backpack stands provocatively in the doorway.

ADRIAN: Oh, *hello.*

MARISSA: Are you Adrian Fuller, the famous writer?

ADRIAN: Yes, I'm, Adrian Fuller, but it's not up to me to say whether or not I'm famous. And who might you be?

MARISSA: Oh, it's very important that I see you. May I come in?

ADRIAN: If it's really that important…please do.

MARISSA: Wow, I simply cannot *believe* it. Here I am... on Capri... with *the* Adrian Fuller!

ADRIAN: Pleased to meet you, Ms...Ms...what did you say your name is?

MARISSA: I didn't. I'm Marissa Portland, but you can call me Marissa. I sent you a letter a few days ago.

ADRIAN: What letter?

MARISSA: A letter about interviewing you. I wrote that I'd come by today. I'm not imposing, am I?

ADRIAN: *(He goes to his desk, flips through papers and finds the letter.)* Oh, so that's you. Look, I'm rather busy, but I'll gladly make an exception. Maybe we could...?

MARISSA: *(She gazes about the room in awe.)* So, this is where it all *happens*!

ADRIAN: What happens?

MARISSA: Where you write your brilliant psychological thrillers!

ADRIAN: I've actually only been here for the past four years...so...

MARISSA: I know. I know *everything*.

ADRIAN: You do, do you...?

MARISSA: Of course. As I mentioned in my letter, I'm writing my doctoral thesis about you and your work.

ADRIAN: My dear Miranda...

MARISSA: Marissa...my name is Marissa.

ADRIAN: Sorry. *(In a vain tone)* My dear Marissa, have you any idea how many articles and papers about me have already been written?

MARISSA: Adrian...may I call you Adrian?

ADRIAN: All right. I call you M...Marissa.

MARISSA: Adrian, I'm perfectly aware of all that's been written about you, but those articles and papers don't have the *unique* perspective that my thesis has.

ADRIAN: And what makes you so sure about that?

MARISSA: *(She goes to the window and takes a deep breath.)* Ahhh...if only I could assimilate this scene...make it part of my body and soul. It is so absolutely breath-taking... *(smiling seductively at ADRIAN)* How can you live here and not... melt? It's like being in paradise.

ADRIAN: One gets used to it.

MARISSA: You seem so nonchalant about your surroundings. Funny, that's exactly how I pictured you.

ADRIAN: Is that so? I guess you don't know me very well.

MARISSA: Oh, but I *do*! Much more than you think.

ADRIAN: What do you mean by that?

MARISSA: I mean, I've gotten to know you through your work, of course. You reveal yourself through your writing, the characters you create, the stories you tell.

ADRIAN: My dear...umm...Marissa, you must realise that a writer has many personas. Who can possibly tell who the *real* Adrian Fuller is? Sometimes even I don't know. Now what makes this...this thesis of yours so unique?

MARISSA: *(Goes up to ADRIAN and lightly touches his arm)* For one thing, my *focus*...

ADRIAN: And pray tell, what is so special about your so-called focus?

MARISSA: I've approached your novels from the point of view of the *women* in them.

ADRIAN: *(Surprised)* The women? That is rather an interesting point of view.

MARISSA: Yes, and how each of these female characters is...how should I put it...is...is... *done away with*, all three of them.

ADRIAN: Three? Why three?

MARISSA: You've published three novels, haven't you? And each one of them is centred on the death of a young female victim.

ADRIAN: I don't think the age and sex of the victims in my novels are particularly relevant. Besides, at the risk of sounding chauvinist, it's a mere coincidence that my victims happen to have been young females.

MARISSA: Adrian, would you mind if I remove my backpack? It's starting to feel a bit heavy.

ADRIAN: Not at all. Be my guest.

MARISSA: *(She places backpack in front of the sideboard and turns toward ADRIAN)* You know, what I find particularly compelling about these three young women is the original *way* in which you have each one murdered. *(She strolls over to the laptop.)* Are you working on number four?

ADRIAN: Hey, I don't allow anyone, not even an attractive doctoral student, to poke their nose into what I am presently writing! *(He shuts the lid of the laptop.)* You, my dear, will just have to wait until the novel is published and available in bookshops.

MARISSA: I *am* sorry. I didn't want to pry.

ADRIAN: Writers have many quirks and one of them is not to divulge even a titbit of information about the latest project they're working on. It...it kills the Muse.

MARISSA: It's interesting you should use that phrase.

ADRIAN: What phrase?

MARISSA: *Kills*...kills the *Muse*.

ADRIAN: It's only a figure of speech. It doesn't signify anything.

MARISSA: But that's exactly what happens in your first novel, "*The Wayward Wife*". What a superb debut! The critics raved about it, and you became famous overnight.

ADRIAN: More luck than skill.

MARISSA: Oh, don't be so modest. I'm sure you were in complete command of your material.

ADRIAN: It was more like stumbling about in the dark until I found the light.

ADRIAN sits down at his desk.

MARISSA: I don't believe you, not with such an ingenious plot. Harold, an artist, is in love with his beautiful young wife, Amelia. She is the Muse who inspires him to paint. And then he discovers that she's having a torrid affair with Rupert, the art critic who hates Harold's paintings! Harold feels betrayed and secretly starts forming a plot to poison Amelia.

ADRIAN: Yes, he's insanely jealous, but manages to conceal it from both of them.

MARISSA: And how he poisons her is so...so *original*.

ADRIAN: I'm glad you like it.

MARISSA: Oh my god, it just blew my mind how Harold uses *cadmium*, one of the pigments that make his paintings so brilliant. He slowly starts to add tiny doses of cadmium to Amelia's meals.

ADRIAN: *Yes*, she grows ill and gradually wastes away.

MARISSA: And no one ever *suspects* Harold.

ADRIAN: Not even his enemy Rupert.

MARISSA: The perfect crime! How do you know so much about toxic pigments? Are you a painter as well as a writer?

ADRIAN: When I was young, I dabbled in art, but didn't have much talent. Are you interested in art?

MARISSA: I *adore* art! I was in Florence yesterday at the Uffizi Gallery, and was absolutely *enthralled* by the Caravaggios...especially...

ADRIAN: I bet it's...it's...*The Shield with the Head of Medusa*!

MARISSA: Do you know it?

ADRIAN: *(He gets up from his desk and going towards MARISSA)* That's the painting where Perseus cuts off the Medusa's head with his sword.

He makes a sweeping gesture with his hand.

MARISSA: Yes, he uses his shiny metal shield like a mirror to find her before she can turn him to *stone. (She sits on the edge of his desk.)* Wow, turning men to stone by *staring* at them – what a thrilling thought!

ADRIAN: Rather chilling, I'd say.

MARISSA: It's primeval female power. I love those writhing snakes on the Medusa's head. *(Stares hard at ADRIAN, then puts her hands on her head, wriggles with her fingers like snakes and cackles)* Are you afraid of women, Adrian?

ADRIAN: Of women like that, yes. *(Looking at her again)* Are You... umm... travelling with anyone?

MARISSA: I *always* travel alone.

ADRIAN: So do I! Makes it easier to meet new people, to embark on new adventures.

MARISSA: I quite agree. Being alone in a foreign place where no one knows you frees the spirit and loosens inhibitions. *(Jumping up from desk and waking about room.)* But let's get back to your books. Where do you find your ideas?

ADRIAN: I take long walks and talk to myself. I also keep a running diary of what I see and think.

MARISSA: Doesn't it bother you?

ADRIAN: What?

MARISSA: Always thinking about ways to *murder* people?

ADRIAN: Doesn't it bother you to read books and watch films about murder?

MARISSA: Touché! It seems like people are *obsessed* with murder mysteries. Perhaps it's because there is a potential murderer in each one of us.

ADRIAN: You might be right. Is there one in you?

MARISSA: Who knows? Perhaps time will tell. (*Turning to ADRIAN so that they are face-to-face.*) You came to Capri because of your wife, didn't you?

ADRIAN: Yes, I came here shortly after she died. I had to get away from London – too much pain and sadness.

MARISSA: I understand. Pain and sadness can be overwhelming. It must have been awful. Kidneys...wasn't it?

ADRIAN: What?

MARISSA: Your wife...she died of a lingering kidney disease, didn't she?

ADRIAN: How do you know that?

MARISSA: Through my research – I must have read it in some newspaper. After that you came to Capri and started to work on "*Missing Evidence*", your second book.

ADRIAN: You really do know a lot about me. Yes, I started writing that book almost four years ago. It was cathartic and helped me get over my grief.

MARISSA: And what a success that book was! Nobody wanted to believe you could write a more gripping novel than your first one.

ADRIAN: After one major success, the critics are usually merciless. So, I had to work really hard on that book. I was basically competing against myself.

MARISSA: Your books got better, and your plots more complicated. You've even been compared to Agatha Christie. Of course, you're not a *Queen of Crime*, are you? (*She laughs.*) May I sit down?

ADRIAN: Make yourself comfortable. May I offer you something to drink?

MARISSA: (*She eases herself into the armchair*). That would be lovely. What do you have?

ADRIAN: *(He goes to the sideboard and holds up one of the bottles.)* A nice local red wine from a vineyard near the ruins of the Villa Jovis...

MARISSA: The *Villa Jovis*! Isn't that where the Roman Emperor Tiberius spent the last years of his life?

ADRIAN: Yes, about eleven years.

MARISSA: Now he was another *monster*...

ADRIAN: *Another* monster?

MARISSA: I'm assuming there are others on the island. Capri is known for attracting bad people, even members of the Mafiosi. So why was Tiberius considered to be such a despicable monster?

ADRIAN: It was his rather annoying habit of having enemies thrown over the highest cliff to sharks circling in the water below, among other nasty little things. *(He pours wine into his glass and fills one for MARISSA.)* Here you are. To your thesis.

MARISSA: And to the success of your next book. May the critics and the public love it!

They clink glasses. ADRIAN sits down at his desk and faces MARISSA.

MARISSA: Mmmm... this wine is delicious! I shouldn't be drinking it though, should I?

ADRIAN: Why not?

MARISSA: Well, what with your habit of bringing young women to an early demise?

ADRIAN: *(Laughing)* That's only in my fiction. I have no intention of poisoning someone who is writing a doctoral thesis about me.

MARISSA: I was actually thinking about Laura, the victim in your second book, "*Missing Evidence*". You killed her off with wine. Or, to be more precise, you murdered her in a *wine cellar*.

ADRIAN: I wish you would stop saying *I* did it. It was the character *Everett* who did it – because he was after his wife's inheritance.

MARISSA: I *am* sorry, Adrian. I didn't want to imply that *you* personally killed Laura. Of course not. As you said, it's only fiction. But asphyxiating her by exposure to the carbon dioxide fumes of fermenting grapes – that is *devilishly* clever! No wonder you called the book "*Missing Evidence*". It was merely a matter of trapping poor Laura in the wine cellar with no ventilation. No one suspected that it was *you*...I mean Everett, an unsuccessful but ambitious novelist, who is the murderer.

A moment of embarrassing silence.

ADRIAN: *(He glances at his watch.)* Look, I think we need to wrap up this interview. I must get back to work. Is there anything else you urgently need to know?

MARISSA: Actually, I have a few more questions about your third book, "*Poetic Injustice*". A few months ago, I bought a copy and couldn't put it down. It was so chillingly realistic that it gave me nightmares.

ADRIAN: *(He goes to sideboard, picks up the book, quickly signs it and hands it to MARISSA.)* Here you are – a signed copy.

MARISSA: Oh, thank you! (*Looks at photo of ADRIAN on back page*) I must say this picture doesn't do you justice at all. You're far more handsome in real life!

ADRIAN: I'm afraid that I'm not very photogenic.

MARISSA: You also actually look much younger.

ADRIAN: You don't think I'm going too grey?

MARISSA: Not at all. It makes you look very distinguished.

ADRIAN: Oh, thank you.

MARISSA: In this your third book you didn't use poison or asphyxiation as a way of doing away with your poor victim.

ADRIAN: What are you getting at?

MARISSA: Sabina, the victim in "*Poetic Injustice*". You got rid of her in such a completely different way.

ADRIAN: Mustn't be repetitive, must one?

MARISSA: (*She turning, peering out the window.*) Oh, I see another boat is arriving, just like the one that came here fifteen months ago.

ADRIAN: (*Puzzled*) What's so special about fifteen months ago?

MARISSA: Oh, nothing. That's just when my older sister came to Capri on holiday. But let's get back to that third book of yours. As I mentioned, the victim isn't poisoned, but *drowned*. Poor Sabina, a young, beautiful art student with her whole life ahead of her. She's in Italy on holiday, staying in Lerici, a town on the north-western coast of Liguria. There she meets the handsome Roland Aubrey, without suspecting that he is a *psychopath*. She falls in love with him. One moonlit night they go sailing in the Bay of La Spezia, but she never returns. (*Pause, turning towards ADRIAN*) You are obsessed with the arts, aren't you?

ADRIAN: I wasn't aware of it. Perhaps I am.

MARISSA: You *are*, and you're also a hopeless Romantic at heart.

ADRIAN: Perhaps I am that too.

MARISSA: Your books are full of references to art and literature. How clever of you to set the scene in La Spezia, also known as the Bay of Poets. That's where Lord Byron swam across the bay and poor Percy Shelley drowned back in 1822. (*She picks up the bottle of wine from the sideboard.*) This wine is *so* delicious. I'd really love to have another glass. There's something distinctive about it – earthy with a hint of the *sinister.*

ADRIAN: Help yourself. Maybe the evil spirit of Tiberius lurks in it.

MARISSA: (*She pours herself another glass of wine*). What about you, Adrian? Do you want another glass?

ADRIAN: Are you trying to get me drunk?

MARISSA: Isn't it usually the other way around?

ADRIAN: What are you saying?

MARISSA: Middle-aged man trying to get young woman tipsy and then...

ADRIAN: You know, I have a lot of work to do and have no intention of getting you tipsy!

MARISSA: Come on, let's have just one more glass to celebrate our meeting. Then I promise to leave and never ever bother you again. (*Places her hand over her heart*) Cross my heart...and hope...*not to...die.*

ADRIAN: All right...but only half a glass. I must keep a clear head.

MARISSA: (*She takes ADRIAN's glass back to the sideboard and slowly fills it.*) I'm sure you can hold your liquor. (*Turning towards ADRIAN.*) Most writers are alcoholics, aren't they?

ADRIAN: I beg your pardon; I am certainly *not* an alcoholic!

MARISSA: Dear, dear Adrian don't take it personally. I meant writers in general.

MARISSA walks back to ADRIAN with her glass and hands him his glass.

ADRIAN: Whoa, I said only half a glass!

MARISSA: You can take it! Here's to art, literature, and *murder. (They clink glasses again, looking into each other's eyes.)* C'mon, let's do a bottoms-up – to our interview! (*Gulps her wine.*)

ADRIAN: All right, if you insist. To our interview! (*Gulps his wine.*) Ugh...this wine tastes really off.

MARISSA: Must be dregs from the bottom of the bottle.

ADRIAN starts to become unsteady on his feet.

ADRIAN: Look, I think it's time for you to go. Let me show you to the door.

MARISSA: I have one more question.

ADRIAN: (*Swaying*) Wh...what?

MARISSA: It wasn't in the Bay of La Spezia, was it?

ADRIAN: I don't know what you mean.

MARISSA: That she drowned.

ADRIAN: What are you talking about?

MARISSA: My sister, Miranda. (*Pointing towards the window.*) She drowned in the Bay of Naples, didn't she?

ADRIAN: (*Clutching at his throat.*) Who...who are you?

MARISSA: (*Getting up close to ADRIAN*) Is there something familiar about these eyes? Are they the same colour, the same shape as my sister's? You see, my real name isn't Marissa Portland, but Barrett, *Barrett*. Does this name sound familiar? Does it ring a bell?

ADRIAN: Oh, no...no...!

She takes the wine glass from his hand and puts it on the desk, then turns and goes up close to him.

MARISSA: Oh, yes, Adrian, and a year ago you took my sister, Miranda Barrett, sailing, didn't you? Was it also on a moonlit night when you pushed her overboard? (*Pushes him down on the chair.*) Did you get her drunk? Did she struggle? (*Shouting.*) Did she cry for help before the waves closed over her head? I want to hear you admit it. I want to know why you did it!

ADRIAN: It was an *accident*! Miranda fell overboard...I didn't kill her.

MARISSA: (*Pushing him down on the floor.*) You lie very badly, Adrian. I know you killed my sister and now you're going to have to pay for your wretched crime.

ADRIAN: This wine...what's wrong with this wine?

She moves up close to ADRIAN as he staggers towards his desk.

MARISSA: I added a little something to spice it up. Of course, nothing as original as in your books. Just a wee pinch of...quite ordinary *cyanide*. The good old-fashioned way.

ADRIAN: *(He flops down at his desk)* No... no...

MARISSA: Yes, Adrian. Now the score is settled, isn't it? All these women who died in your books... you killed them in *real* life, including your wife.

ADRIAN: I did *not* kill my wife!

MARISSA: She had a lot of money but refused to give you any. You tried to earn your own living as a writer, but you were not really all that good. The simple truth, Adrian, is you were drying up and soon you would be just a penniless *has been*!

ADRIAN: *(Staring at her as she goes to the laptop)* I...I...

MARISSA: And you murdered all these women so that you could savour the *realistic* effect. Let's face it, Adrian, you never had any imagination and could only write about what you experienced first-hand. How sick! *(Moving very close to ADRIAN)* Now, how does it *feel* to be one of your own characters facing imminent demise – in *real* time?

ADRIAN: *(Gasping)* You...you de...de...vil...

MARISSA: *(Bending over the laptop)* What a pity you can't finish your last novel. You know, your books taught me a lot about eliminating clues and covering up tracks, so I'm taking my letter with me. *(Grabs letter)* And then there are fingerprints. Mustn't leave any fingerprints behind, must one? *(She takes a handkerchief from the pocket of her jacket, wipes the neck of the bottle and the stem of ADRIAN's wine glass, and then puts them next to him.)* This will make it look like a suicide. I'll take my glass and your book with me. *(Sticks glass and book into backpack, straps it on and is ready to leave)* That should do it. *(Heads for the door, then turns)* Ooops, I almost forget. There are some of my fingerprints on the armchair and sideboard. *(Wipes armchair and sideboard)* And even on your arm. *(Flicks her handkerchief across his arm)*. Now everything is neat and tidy. *(She goes to the door, turns back)* Bye-bye, Adrian. I really must catch my boat. *Die well*!

ADRIAN stares after her, then slumps over desk. Silence, as the light slowly dims. This time a mournful version of "'Twas on the Isle of Capri" is played, with the second stanza included. It can be recorded by the main actress or someone else, without orchestral accompaniment.

'Twas on the Isle of Capri that I found her.

Beneath the shade of an old walnut tree

Oh, I can still see the flowers blooming round her.

Where we met on the Isle of Capri.She was as sweet as a rose at the dawning

But somehow fate hadn't meant her for me.

And though I sailed with the tide in the morning

Still my heart's on the Isle of Capri...

Pause

ADRIAN: *(Raising his head from desk as lights go back on)*. I've got it...I've finally got the perfect end for my book! (*Eagerly starts typing*) As Marissa leaves, she turns back and says, "Bye-bye, Adrian. I really must catch my boat. *Die well!*" (*pause*) I think I'll call it... Capri. (*Thoughtful.*) Yes, *Capri*.

END

5

About the Author

Roger Bonner

Roger Bonner is a Swiss author and poet who grew up in Los Angeles, California. He has written two books: *Swiss Me*, a collection of humorous columns written for various magazines and books about adapting to life in Switzerland, and *The Lost Treasure of the Swiss Alps*, an adventure story for kids and adults.

Capri is the second of three popular short plays he has written for the Semi-Circle Theatre in Basel, Switzerland. The play won two nominations (best actress and original script) and an award for best visual ending at the 2023 Festival of European Anglophone Theatrical Societies (FEATS) in Bad Homburg, Germany.

The theatre bug has bitten him, and he plans to write more plays.

www.roger-bonner.ch

6

Tortive Lit

www.tortivelit.com

Tortive Lit is part of Tortive Theatre Ltd.

We publish play scripts from writers at all stages of their careers and provide a home for new stories through our competitions and online short story publications.

We are dedicated to promoting emerging writers and original storytelling. Our platform is a space for innovative literary work, connecting writers with readers and fostering a community of literary enthusiasts, especially in the world of theatre.

We are committed to showcasing diverse voices and supporting the development of new literary talent.

For more information please visit www.tortivelit.com

www.ingramcontent.com/pod-product-compliance
Lightning Source LLC
Chambersburg PA
CBHW071237170626
46809CB00008BA/3105